Procrastination

Deal with it all in good time

Diane Peters • Illustrated by Jeremy Tankard

James Lorimer & Company Ltd., Publishers
Toronto

It's six o'clock, and you're in big trouble.

Your mom is about to walk through the door and your room isn't clean — again. You promised that it would be spotless when she got home from work, but you spent the entire afternoon playing video games, talking on the phone, and eating snacks. All you've done is put one pair of socks in your laundry basket.

You've been procrastinating.

Most people have stuff they tend to put off. But when you miss deadlines, break promises, or delay doing something until the last minute — especially on a regular basis — you can create a lot of stress and conflict in your life.

There are many reasons why we procrastinate. Maybe we're tired or what we have to do is really difficult. We might think we can do a better job if we take more time. Whatever the reason, procrastinating can cause trouble and make it hard for others to trust us.

Some people never, ever put things off.

No matter how impossible the deadline, they'll push themselves to do things on time. This is a kind of perfectionism, or always trying to do things perfectly. Perfectionists may put a lot of pressure on themselves. They may also get into conflicts with people who are more relaxed about schedules.

Both procrastination and perfectionism happen for many reasons, but a popular one is being afraid to fail. Could that be why *you* put things off or knock yourself out to meet deadlines? Whatever the reason, if getting things done on time creates problems in your life, this book can help.

Contents

What is

Everyone knows about procrastinating, right?

It's when we put things off until the very last minute — or don't do them at all. It's easy to see that there are lots of things you'd rather be up to than:

- doing homework
- cleaning your room, closet, or locker
- getting to your household chores
- studying for exams or tests
- running an errand

Procrastination?

But sometimes we put off things that should be easy and take no time at all. Have you ever delayed or bailed when you had to:

- write a sensitive e-mail or letter?
- apologize to someone?
- face someone who's mad at you or you're mad at?
- deal with money, like repaying a loan or asking for a bigger allowance?
- finish up something you'd already put a lot of time and effort into?
- buy a gift or a card?
- write a thank-you note?
- tell someone how you really feel?

Whether something is hard to do or you just don't know how to go about it, putting it off is procrastinating. And the worst thing about it? Procrastination usually means more stress and work than if you'd just got the thing over with straight away.

Procrastination 101

Hey, it's easy to avoid doing

The next day...
You still haven't said anything to Arooj?
No, but I will.
You two are real friends. Unlike some people.

something...

Let's hang out.
Seriously? You must be done the project already.
On the day of the deadline...
Oh, Alex. This looks really sloppy and rushed.
Saturday...
Sunday...
HISTORY
This is brutal. And it's going to take all night!
POST OFFICE
OPEN
Later...
You didn't mail it? Oh no! The post office is closed now!

QUIZ

What day are you?

Some people never get to the dreary jobs in life. Are you one of those people who never does today what can be put off until tomorrow? Are you so organized that it seems like everything got done yesterday? Or are you somewhere in between — doing the best you can do today? Take this quiz and check out your behaviour on the next page.

1. It's starting to snow hard, and it's your job to shovel. Do you: a) Do it right away, even if you have to go back out again later? b) Check the forecast and wait until it stops snowing? c) Rush to get it done before school tomorrow morning?

2. Your grandmother bought you a sweater that just doesn't fit and needs to be exchanged. Do you: a) Plan what you'll say before you call, in case you hurt her feelings? b) Just pick up the phone and tell her politely? c) Avoid calling until it's too late to do the exchange?

3. The deadline to apply for a great summer job is three weeks away. Do you: a) Leave it until the night before, and have to drop off the application in person? b) Take your time filling out the application, and mail it off a week before the deadline? c) Fill out the application really quickly and pay extra to get it there right away?

4. You want to reorganize your desk before school starts in the fall. Do you: a) Work on it all day, every day, until it's perfect? b) Finally tackle the mess after the first week of school? c) Set aside a couple of days in August to get organized?

5. You and your siblings are planning an amazing Mother's Day breakfast. It's your job to get a card. Do you: a) Shop around for the best card ever? b) Pick something nice up while you're at the mall? c) Realize while the breakfast is sizzling away that you have to run out to buy whatever card you can find?

6 You love to paint and just bought a huge canvas. Do you: a) Spend a Saturday playing around with your paints? b) Have dreams about a big, empty canvas that you can't bring yourself to touch? c) Put in late nights making sketch after sketch of what you will paint?

7 It's your job to put out the garbage at seven o'clock on Tuesday mornings. Do you: a) Dash out to do your chore every Tuesday at 6:55? b) Organize the bins on Monday mornings and put them out after school? c) After dinner on Monday nights, collect the trash and put it out?

8 You're supposed to pick up your little brother at swimming lessons by noon. Do you: a) Get there at 11:45 and sit in the cold car until he's ready? b) Leave the house late and have to race to the pool? c) Arrive around noon (give or take a few minutes) to get him?

9 Someone will need to cover your paper route when you're at your cousin's wedding in August. Do you: a) Let your boss know in July? b) Forget to tell your boss and end up begging a pal to help you out? c) Tell your boss in March that you've arranged for a replacement?

10 Your bedroom lamp needs a special replacement bulb. Do you: a) Find a replacement bulb before the old one burns out? b) Just use the overhead light, and never replace the bulb in your lamp? c) Get a new light bulb within a week of it burning out?

Answers

1. a) Yesterday
   b) Today
   c) Tomorrow
2. a) Today
   b) Yesterday
   c) Tomorrow
3. a) Tomorrow
   b) Today
   c) Yesterday
4. a) Yesterday
   b) Tomorrow
   c) Today
5. a) Yesterday
   b) Today
   c) Tomorrow
6. a) Today
   b) Tomorrow
   c) Yesterday
7. a) Tomorrow
   b) Yesterday
   c) Today
8. a) Yesterday
   b) Tomorrow
   c) Today
9. a) Today
   b) Tomorrow
   c) Yesterday
10. a) Yesterday
    b) Tomorrow
    c) Today

Dear Conflict Counsellor

Q: I work best when I'm under pressure. What's so bad about putting things off until the heat is on?

— Last Minute

A: Sometimes working close to a deadline can help get you to move quickly to get things done. But let's look at it a different way: are you sure you're not hurting yourself or others? Does your mom get tired of making you midnight snacks? Are you always calling on your friends to help you out at the last minute? Do you ever do a poor job because you've run out of time? If so, maybe being under pressure doesn't help as much as you think.

Q: I just got in a lot of trouble in class. The project I was working on with a partner got left to the last minute, but it wasn't my fault. I was ready to work, but my partner wasn't, and we fell behind. Now my teacher thinks I'm a procrastinator!

— Wrongly Accused

A: It's hard to be called something you're not. When we work on projects with others, the outcome depends on the work habits of everyone involved. Think about what you can do next time to make things go more smoothly. You could talk to your partner early on about a schedule you can both live with. You could inform your teacher before the deadline if you and your partner are having trouble. Sometimes all you can do is take responsibility for your part in getting things done.

Q: I've been called a perfectionist by a lot of people, and they don't mean it nicely. I always do my very best on everything, and I work harder than anyone I know on school projects and at my part-time job. Why do I get put down for it? What's their problem?

— Perfectly Perfect

A: If you are happy with what you're doing, then you shouldn't make their problem yours. But look closely at your life. Are you working that hard because it makes your life happy and keeps it running smoothly or so your friends, parents, or teachers will think you're perfect? And what happens when other people don't meet your high standards? Just be sure you're not being too tough on yourself, missing out on having fun, or causing conflict with others with your "perfect" ways.

Q: I'm really good about getting most of my homework done. But I just can't seem to make time for Science. I keep meaning to, but I never seem to get to it. Is it a mental block?

— Experimental

A: Sometimes, certain subjects or tasks just rub us the wrong way. Think about why it's your Science homework that you always put off. Do you find it boring because it's too easy, or is Science your hardest subject? Do you get frustrated when you try to work through it? Do you have someone you can go to when you need help? Or does there always seem to be just too much of it? Maybe it's got less to do with the homework itself and more to do with something emotional. For example, if you don't do your homework, does that give you an excuse for getting a low grade? Has anyone ever told you, or do you tell yourself, that you don't have a mind for science? Once you work out why you always put off your Science homework, it will probably be easier to find a solution.

Q: I put everything off, and I feel terrible about it. I spend a lot of time thinking about how I let people down by being late with things, and I'm always panicking about something. Does procrastinating make you a bad person?

— Badly Put Off

A: Procrastination is a habit you've developed, but that doesn't make you a bad person. The problem is, if you put things off, sometimes that makes people lose respect for you or get angry with you. That can hurt your self-esteem and make you feel bad about yourself, not just about your bad habits.

Myths

Deadlines are not set in stone.

Some deadlines may be flexible, but many are not. At some point, you may miss an important deadline and that'll be that.

I have it harder than everyone else.

Everyone has to do things they don't want to. Basically, it is as hard as you make it, and putting things off usually makes things harder.

Everyone expects procrastination.

You're half-right. If you procrastinate a lot, people may stop trusting you to get things done. They may also think you don't respect their wishes and feelings when you miss deadlines.

The important thing is that it gets done.

Rushing to do a project right before the deadline causes stress to you and those around you. Plus, you could be short-changing yourself by doing a poor job.

Did You Know?

- According to a U.S. study, 28% of adults procrastinate regularly.
- One study of college students found that 65% wanted to stop

I work best under pressure.

No one does their best work when they are under constant stress. Procrastinating keeps you from building the self-discipline it takes to do a good job all the time.

Never put off until tomorrow what you can do today.

On the whole, this is a great attitude — unless it means that you try to do everything in the universe on the same day! Remember that people will still like and respect you even if you're not perfectly perfect.

All work and no play makes me a dull kid.

Most people feel guilty and stressed out when they procrastinate. Having those feelings probably makes play time a whole lot less fun.

When I procrastinate, I'm only hurting myself.

Your stress and frantic schedule can be upsetting for the people around you. It's hard on others when they feel like they can't depend on you.

putting off essays, 62% wished they studied sooner for exams, and 55% felt they should start assignments earlier.

- Experts say one of the best ways to help perfectionists is to build up their self-esteem.

It's the morning of the big test and you know you've blown it.

You should have started studying weeks ago, but you left all your cramming until the last minute. Now after being up all night you can barely keep your eyes open, much less do well on the exam.

Why do you keep doing this to yourself?

DEAR DR. SHRINK-WRAPPED . . .

Q. I put off everything! It's not that I don't care — seriously — because it happens all the time with things that are important to me. How can I change?

— *Later Gator*

A. The first step towards change is identifying the problem, Later. Dr. Shrink-Wrapped says, "Good for you!" Remember that often people put things off because they are afraid of something. Does that sound like you? The trick to shaking your fears is telling yourself that who you are — the value you have as a person — is not measured by how well you do one thing. If you get a bad grade, it doesn't mean you're stupid, it just means you didn't do great on that test or project. Try these suggestions for facing your fears:

- Talk to friends and family about your feelings and where they might be coming from.
- Ask the people around you to ease up on the pressure.
- Remind yourself regularly that you are a lovable person who is able to do things well.
- Write reassuring notes to yourself and post them around your room.
- Find one or two things that you are good at and use them to boost your ego when you need it.
- Give yourself a break!

Q. I love playing video games. I mean, I really love it. I'm good, too. Problem is, gaming sometimes gets in the way of other stuff I'm supposed to be doing. Does that really matter if I've found something I love to do?

— *Space Invaded*

A. Dr. Shrink-Wrapped thinks it's time for a reality check, Spacey. Part of growing up is learning you can't play all the time. Consider what you gain by getting more balance in your life instead of more points in your fave video game. Wouldn't it be nice to game guilt-free because you've done your work? Wouldn't it be great if people weren't always nagging you about the stuff you're supposed to be doing? And wouldn't it be *awesome* if your grades were good enough to get you into a school where you could learn to design the games you love?

Q. *Shhh.* I have a big secret. I am a closet procrastinator. I don't tell people when I've put things off, so no one knows that I'm not finished or that I'm scrambling to get things done. I've become really good at hiding this, and everyone always tells me how great it is that I'm so on top of things. But I feel like a big fake, and I don't know how much longer I can keep it up.

— *Secretly Stressed*

A. Secretly, I don't know how you cope! You're dealing with two very powerful sources of stress. First, being a procrastinator is difficult, as you're always worrying about projects that aren't done and deadlines that aren't met. But being secretive about your habits makes it even worse. You're likely spending a lot of time — time you could be working on chores or projects — hiding your delaying ways. Dr. Shrink-Wrapped suggest you start slow — come clean with a close friend or trusted adult. Tell them about your problem and have them help you brainstorm ways of getting out of it. Push yourself just a little bit to be more honest and to stick to your plans. With some effort, you can break your secret cycle. And it's no secret how good that will feel!

QUIZ

Are you a putter-offer?

Almost everyone procrastinates sometimes. Take this quiz to find out how you rate on the procrastination scale. Of the following statements, which ones are true about you and which ones false?

1. I get overwhelmed by big tasks.
2. I don't like to ask for help.
3. I like to work on just one thing at a time.
4. I don't like to start things if I'm not sure I can finish.
5. I don't like to start things if I'm not sure they will turn out really well.
6. I find it hard to put work ahead of fun.
7. I'm afraid of doing things wrong.
8. I don't want people to think I'm stupid.
9. I tell people things are okay, even when they're not.
10. It's really hard for me to schedule my time.

I'm very disorganized. 11

I work best when a deadline is closing in. 12

It's hard keeping my attention on my work. 13

I just don't know where the time goes. 14

I don't like being told what to do by others. 15

I find that if I put things off, other people will help me out. 16

I don't see the point in doing things early. 17

I can't work when I'm upset about something. 18

If a task is really boring, I have a hard time forcing myself to do it. 19

I've never suffered really bad consequences from putting something off. 20

So, how did you do? Did you score a lot of trues? Then maybe it's time to admit you have a problem with procrastination. Take a good look at your behaviour, and see if you can improve things for yourself and those around you.

How to Put an End to Putting Things Off

So, there you are again, hiding from your responsibilities. You probably spend a lot of time covering your tracks so no one knows how out of control you feel. Are you ready to put a stop to that cycle of stress? You can, you know, starting *right now*. Here are just a few of the things you can do to take back control of your life.

Schedule yourself. If you write to-do lists for what you should be doing and when, it's much easier to keep yourself on track. You'll also learn to set realistic goals for how long each task should take.

Know your temptations. Do you like to watch TV at night instead of studying? Would you rather play basketball than do your household chores? Figure out which things distract you from work and find ways to limit the temptation. That's not to say you can't ever have fun! Just remember when you're tempted to slack off that you can have worry-free fun *after* the work is done.

Reward yourself. Plan on doing the things you love after you're done work, not as a way of putting it off. And when you do have play time, enjoy it without any guilt.

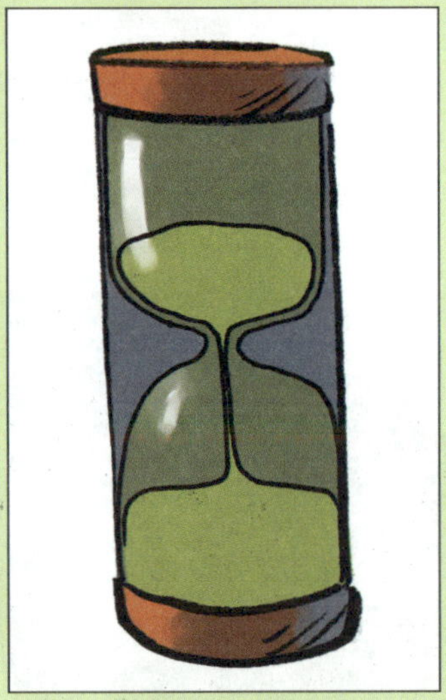

Break it down. If you have a big or difficult project to do, get started by doing just a little — say, five or fifteen minutes — to start. Be sure you understand what is expected of you and what sort of challenges may be ahead.

Get support. Ask your friends and family for help by having them

- not tempt you with fun things when you have work to do
- remind you to get back to your tasks when you go off track
- not step in to help you complete last-minute tasks
- encourage you with positive words and compliments.

Take a moment. If you do find yourself delaying getting to work, stop for a minute and think about why you're doing this. What will the consequences be if you put things off?

DID YOU KNOW?

- Remember those New Year's resolutions? Well, 70% of them are abandoned by February 1.

Get help. Tick off your must-do list with a friend who has similar things that need doing. If a problem, like trouble at home, is making it hard to get things done, tell a trusted adult. Consider getting some counselling to help you through this tough time. Part of being responsible is taking care of yourself, too.

do's and don'ts

- ✓ Do take pride in your work.
- ✓ Do make sure you understand what you're getting into when you offer to do something.
- ✓ Do ask for help if you need it.
- ✓ Do remember that no one is perfect and just try your best.
- ✓ Do talk to others about why you procrastinate.
- ✓ Do plan on completing all projects on time.
- ✓ Do get started right away on things you must do.
- ✓ Do think who will be hurt if you don't finish a task.
- ✓ Do find ways to reward yourself when you finish a tough or unpleasant job.
- ✓ Do take responsibility when you miss a deadline.
- ✗ Don't assume procrastination hurts no one.
- ✗ Don't work on projects you don't understand without asking questions.
- ✗ Don't make light of your procrastination habit.
- ✗ Don't let deadlines be your only motivation.
- ✗ Don't think you're a bad person because you put things off.
- ✗ Don't consider yourself a failure because you did poorly on one thing.
- ✗ Don't put all your feelings of self-worth into one project.
- ✗ Don't keep your stress and anxiety to yourself.

Experts say that many procrastinators can benefit from using to-do lists, schedules, and rewards for work done.

- Studying for just an hour at a time and taking frequent breaks works better than studying for 2 or 3 hours at a time.

No one has anything on you.

You get everything done on time. You show up for work on the dot and every morning you make your bed before you've even rubbed the sleep out of your eyes.

How could anyone have a problem with that?

What's wrong with being perfect?

Well, nothing — or it wouldn't be perfection! The problem is that there's no such thing as absolute perfection: there will always be a flaw.

Has meeting — or beating — deadlines become more important to you than your health or your relationships with other people? When was the last time you cut yourself some slack and had a little fun, or maybe a full night's sleep?

Putting yourself under constant pressure can cause you a lot of stress. It affects the people around you, too. When you're always striving to be number one, you may

- forget to laugh and listen to others
- forget to give yourself time to rest and relax
- stop enjoying the fun things you are interested in
- neglect to spend time with your friends and family

You might also…

- confuse the things you do with your value as a person
- have a hard time being happy for others when they do well and have successes
- get into conflicts with less-driven people
- be at risk of developing an eating disorder, an addiction, or another problem related to stress or perfectionism

Hey, let's not be too rough on the perfectionists here. Striving to do your best is a good thing! It's all about learning to balance work and fun. Funnily enough, sometimes the surest way to be in top form, is to take it easy on yourself.

QUIZ

Can you spot perfection?

Where's the line between a healthy attention to detail and the kind of perfectionism that can make you a total drag? Read the following scenarios and decide whether each is a positive or negative example of being the best. Check your answers on the opposite page.

1. Anita has decided to redecorate her room, and her parents have even given her a budget. She really gets into it — finding fabric samples, looking at paint colours, and organizing her friends to come and help.

2. Final exams are one month away and Phillipe is ready. He's drawn up a strict study schedule. He has informed his soccer coach he'll be missing practices, and his parents that he won't be able to do his regular chores until after exams.

3. Misha decides to make a special lunch for her friend's birthday. She downloads a difficult recipe, and when she accidentally burns the chicken, she ends up in tears.

4. Zack really wants a job at the new store opening up at the mall. He polishes his résumé, and makes sure he looks his best when he drops it off. The day of his interview, he's very nervous.

5. Dale has joined a book club and wants to make a good impression. He not only reads that week's selected book, but all of the author's other books, too.

6. Juanita finally gets the guitar she's always wanted. Every night, once her homework is done, she spends time practising her instrument.

7. Hockey playoffs are just two weeks away and Lloyd doesn't want to miss any practices. Even when he gets a really bad cold, he drags himself out onto the ice. Lloyd ends up giving his cold to a teammate.

8. Anna must write an essay about her dreams and aspirations. A month before it's due, she has already written several drafts of the essay, and still worries it won't be good enough.

9. Gareth has just landed a part in the school play, and he sets aside a weekend to learn his lines. When his pals ask him out to a movie, he says he'll have to skip it this time.

10. Two weeks before the family leaves for the cottage, Emily has already started packing. She has a long to-do list and keeps picking up things for the trip when she's at the mall with her friends.

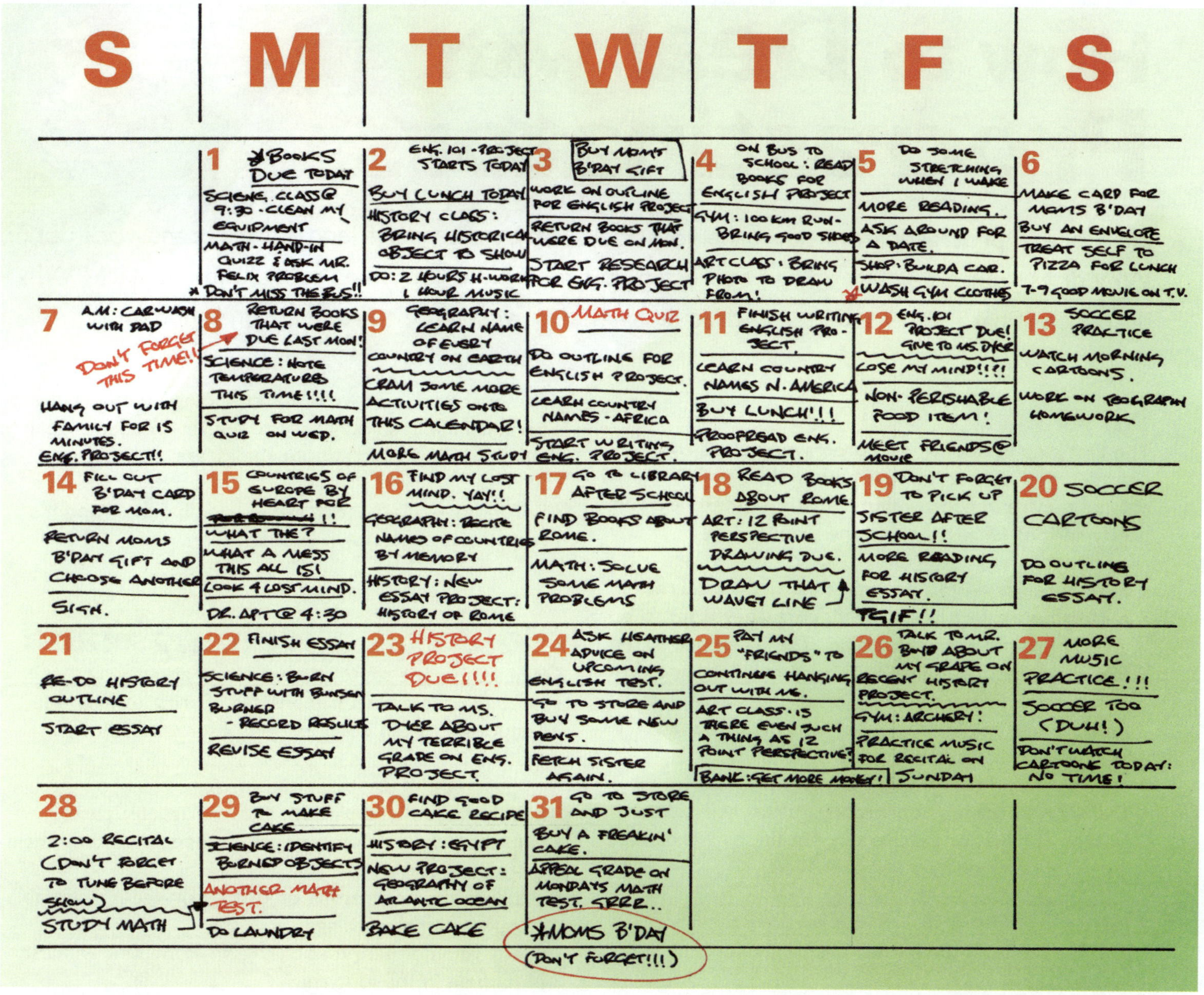

Answers

1. Positive. Anita's passionate about a project, enjoying herself, and sharing the fun.
2. Negative. Phillipe is forgetting to have balance in his life and ignoring his other commitments.
3. Negative. Misha has put so much pressure on herself, she cannot cope with her mistakes.
4. Positive. Zack has done his best to land the job, and being nervous is normal.
5. Negative. It's okay if Dale enjoys reading all those books, but it seems like he is mostly concerned with appearing smart at the meeting.
6. Positive. Juanita has her priorities straight, doing her homework first, then playing guitar.
7. Negative. If Lloyd had been easier on himself, his team would have been better off.
8. Negative. Anna is clearly driven to work so hard by her fear of failure.
9. Positive. Gareth will enjoy time with his friends again once his lines are memorized.
10. Positive. Emily's on top of her to-do list, but not letting it stop her from seeing her friends.

How to Deal with Procrastinators

Let's face it, procrastinators can make you crazy. Why can't your friend get his homework done? Why does your sister bail on her chores so that the whole family has to pick up the slack? Why do procrastinators make things so difficult for themselves and everyone around them?

Find the Feeling

The first step in dealing with procrastinators is to consider why they are always putting things off. They may act like they're in control, but sometimes there are some pretty serious feelings behind the scenes.

- Fear of failure — Many procrastinators are secret perfectionists. Just like perfectionists, they want to do a good job and are afraid to fail. The difference is, this fear drives perfectionists to work extra hard and do things early. Procrastinators, on the other hand, may let their fear get in the way of starting. If you haven't started, you haven't failed yet, right?

- Defiance — Some people rebel against their parents, bosses, families, or teachers by not finishing projects on time, or by doing a half-baked job.

- Feeling overwhelmed — Sometimes the bigger or tougher the task, the harder it is to get started.

- Exhaustion — Putting things off can be really stressful and tiring. And when another deadline comes along, a procrastinator may not have the energy to plan out the work and get started on time.

- Bad planning — Lots of people are, by nature, not so great at organizing their time. Deadlines creep up on them, they fall behind, and they get caught in a procrastination cycle.

- Personal stuff — If we're upset about something in our personal life, it's really hard to get the mind into gear to write an essay or clean out the garage.

- Boredom — Some jobs are dull, dull, dull — and it's really hard to sit down and do them.

Hold out a Helping Hand

Once you've got some understanding about why someone procrastinates, consider offering to help out. That doesn't mean doing the work for them! But you might

- help break down a big task into manageable parts
- help the procrastinator create a schedule to keep their tasks on track
- reassure the procrastinator that he or she is really able to take control of things
- gently remind them that bailing on something will just hurt them in the long run
- make a game or competition out of a boring task, or do your work together
- suggest the procrastinator talk to a trusted adult if there is a life problem that makes it hard to concentrate on other things.

DID YOU KNOW?

- A study out of Carleton University in Ottawa found that students who tend to procrastinate have more digestive problems and sleep disorders.

do's and don'ts

- ✓ Do give yourself permission to fail sometimes.
- ✓ Do applaud others who do well.
- ✓ Do give yourself some time off.

- ✓ Do enjoy the tasks that mean something to you.
- ✓ Do delegate jobs to others and accept what they accomplish.

- ✓ Do cooperate with others when you're working together.
- ✓ Do work hard, but within reason.
- ✓ Do try to achieve balance in your life.

- ✗ Don't believe that perfection exists.
- ✗ Don't stay up late working on projects.
- ✗ Don't stress out over small tasks.

- ✗ Don't equate your self-worth with the things you do.
- ✗ Don't boss others around.
- ✗ Don't lose your sense of fun.
- ✗ Don't become obsessed with work or projects.

- Procrastinators are also more likely to get very sick when they come down with a cold or the flu.
- The same study found that procrastinators smoke, drink, and use drugs more than people who don't procrastinate.

Your sister's big sweet sixteen

birthday party was three weeks ago. You've just spotted your mother — who's clearly tired of nagging your sister to do it — writing the thank-you cards herself. It really steams you that your sister managed to weasel out of something she was supposed to do.

What can you do?

Not a victimless crime

When someone procrastinates, it may hurt their friends, family, and classmates by

- making them feel like they should pitch in
- forcing them to pick up the slack while the procrastinator scrambles to get something done
- pressuring them to cover up for the procrastinator
- causing them to worry on the procrastinator's behalf
- upsetting their schedules for getting projects done
- spoiling plans to go out and have fun
- causing them to distrust and resent the person.

do's and don'ts

✓ Do make sure your own needs are being met.

✓ Do voice your feelings when someone has let you or others down.

✓ Do tell a trusted adult if others are being hurt by someone's procrastination.

✓ Do stay focused on your own projects and deadlines.

✓ Do remind procrastinators that they are valuable, no matter what they accomplish.

✓ Do walk away if you're being taken advantage of.

✗ Don't help those who put things off by taking over tasks they are responsible for.

✗ Don't seek revenge.

✗ Don't cover up someone else's irresponsibility.

✗ Don't procrastinate because others get away with it.

✗ Don't blame yourself when someone else is disorganized.

✗ Don't nag a procrastinator to get back to work.

✗ Don't start to feel out of control.

✗ Don't take on someone else's stress or anxiety.

QUIZ

Help out or walk away?

It's hard to know what to do when someone you know procrastinates and it starts affecting the people around them. But you do have choices! What would you do in the following situations? This quiz has no right or wrong answers, because each situation — and every person — is different. Your answers might be different from the ones suggested here, but they could be right under the circumstances.

1 PROJECT PROBLEMS

You're working on a group project at school. The person who is supposed to write up the bibliography has procrastinated. It's the day before the deadline, and you find out he's not done, but everyone else is ready to hand in their parts.

- Call a meeting to have everyone report on their progress.
- Hand in your project with no bibliography or an incomplete one. This is a group project and, while everyone will lose marks, it's just a project.
- Discuss with the group how you'll tell the teacher why there's no bibliography.

2 GARBAGE DUMP

It's your sister's job to take out the garbage every week. But she's always got an excuse for why it's not done. Half the time, your mom buys it and she's the one who has to drag the garbage to the curb.

- Tell your mom you feel this is unfair to her and unfair to you, as you always do your chores and don't get extra help.
- Talk to your sister and tell her how you feel about her not doing her chores on time.

3 Future Fears

Your best friend hands in all his school projects late. His marks are really starting to slide. You're pretty sure he could fail the year because of his procrastination.

- Tell him, in private, that you're worried about him.
- Offer to help him get organized.
- Suggest an understanding teacher he could talk to about getting caught up with his schoolwork.

4 HEARTBREAKER

Your best buddy never really breaks up with a girl before he starts dating another. He'll say, "Oh yeah, I'll call her," but he never does. Sometimes you feel so bad for the girl, you end up doing his dirty work for him.

- Refuse to keep cleaning up your friend's messes.
- If his ex-girlfriends come to you, tell them where your friend is so they can confront him.
- Tell your friend that he is creating a lot of hurt feelings.

5 Deadline Dad

Your dad is late for everything. He's hardly ever on time to pick you up after soccer practice. And when it's his turn to make dinner, the family doesn't eat until so late that everyone is starving.

- Try to arrange your life so you're not relying on your dad to be on time.
- Tell him how it makes you feel to be left waiting or hungry.
- Draw up a schedule for the whole family.

Continues . . .

6 COMPUTER CON

One of your teachers likes homework submitted by e-mail, and your classmate has worked out quite a scam. She can change the time on her computer clock so late assignments look like they arrived on time.

- Tell her how you feel about her trickery and ask her to stop.
- Let it go. The teacher will figure it out eventually.
- Don't be tempted to do the same thing.

7 Lab Liability

Your science lab partner never does her share of the work on time. Each week, her part of the lab report is either scribbled in at the last minute, or handed in late.

- Have a talk with your lab partner about how her late work is affecting your marks.
- Map out a solution together, like setting early deadlines.
- Talk with your teacher about the problems you've been having with your lab partner.

8 Unscheduled

Every week your boss posts the schedule at the last minute, which makes it hard for you and your coworkers to make plans. It bugs you when your boss takes long coffee breaks before the schedule is finished.

- Politely tell your boss how you feel.
- Ask your boss to call a staff meeting to discuss a new approach to the schedule.
- If the problem continues, inform your boss's boss (if she has one) about what's going on.

DID YOU KNOW?

- About 70% of university students are habitual procrastinators.

9 CHORE AND CHORE ALIKE

You share a room with your sister. Almost every day, you end up making the beds and picking up dirty laundry just so you can stand it in there. When your parents send you both to do a serious clean up, she gets on the phone and you do all the work.

- Tell your sister calmly how you feel about her mess.
- Tidy only your side of the room. She'll either get found out or will start making efforts to make the place livable.
- Call a family meeting to discuss the situation.

10 CARPOOL CHAOS

You carpool to school every day with a friend. On the days he drives, he's always late. You've started to get into trouble because you're never on time for your first-period class.

- Set an earlier departure time for school that will get you there on time, even if your friend is late.
- Help your friend find solutions for getting ready on time.
- Consider finding another person to carpool with.

- Statistics show that … more than 75% of graduate Social Studies students experience anxiety when faced with studying statistics in school.

Two types of procrastinators:
- those who love the rush of doing something late
- avoiders who fear failing

More **Help**

It takes time and practice to learn the skills in this book. There are many ways to deal with procrastination, but only you know what feels right for you in different situations. In the end, the best response is the one that keeps your life running most smoothly.

If you need more information or someone to talk to, these resources might help.

Helplines

Kids Help Phone (Canada) 1-800-668-6868

Youth Crisis Hotline (USA) 1-800-448-4663

Web sites

Canadian Safe Schools Network: www.cssn.org

Kids Help Phone: www.kidshelp.sympatico.ca

Books

Jesse's Star by Ellen Schwartz. Orca Book Publishers, 2000.

Making the Grade by H.G. Sotzek. Vanwell, 2003.

Off Track by Bill Swan. James Lorimer & Company, 2003.

Rooster by Don Trembath. Orca, 2005.

Soccer Star by Jacqueline Guest. Lorimer, 2003.

Too Many Men by Lorna Schultz Nicholson. Lorimer, 2006.

Walking A Thin Line by Sylvia McNicoll. Scholastic Canada, 1997.

Water Fight! by Michele Martin Bossley. Lorimer, 1996.

The Wizzle War by Gordon Korman. Scholastic, 2003.

Other titles in the Deal With It series:

Arguing: Deal with it word by word by Elaine Slavens, illustrated by Steven Murray.

Authority: Deal with it before it deals with you by Anne Marie Aikins, illustrated by Steven Murray.

Bullying: Deal with it before push comes to shove by Elaine Slavens, illustrated by Brooke Kerrigan.

Competition: Deal with it from start to finish by Mireille Messier, illustrated by Steven Murray.

Fighting: Deal with it without coming to blows by Elaine Slavens, illustrated by Steven Murray.

Girlness: Deal with it body and soul by Diane Peters, illustrated by Steven Murray.

Gossip: Deal with it before word gets around by Catherine Rondina, illustrated by Dan Workman.

Guyness: Deal with it body and soul by Steve Pitt, illustrated by Steven Murray.

Lying: Deal with it straight up by Catherine Rondina, illustrated by Dan Workman.

Misconduct: Deal with it without bending the rules by Anne Marie Aikins, illustrated by Steven Murray.

Peer Pressure: Deal with it without losing your cool by Elaine Slavens, illustrated by Ben Shannon.

Privacy: Deal with it like nobody's business by Diane Peters, illustrated by Jeremy Tankard.

Racism: Deal with it before it gets under your skin by Anne Marie Aikins, illustrated by Steven Murray.

Rudeness: Deal with it if you please by Catherine Rondina, illustrated by Dan Workman.

Teasing: Deal with it before the joke's on you by Steve Pitt, illustrated by Remie Geoffroi.

James Lorimer & Company Ltd. acknowledges the support of the Ontario Arts Council. We acknowledge the support of the Government of Canada through the Book Publishing Industry Development Program (BPIDP) for our publishing activities. We acknowledge the support of the Canada Council for the Arts for our publishing program. We acknowledge the support of the Government of Ontario through the Ontario Media Development Corporation's Ontario Book Initiative.

The Canada Council for the Arts | Le Conseil des Arts du Canada

40 YEARS · 40 ANS
ONTARIO ARTS COUNCIL
CONSEIL DES ARTS DE L'ONTARIO

Series design: Blair Kerrigan/Glyphics

Library and Archives Canada Cataloguing in Publication

Peters, Diane
Procrastination : deal with it all in good time / Diane Peters ; illustrated by Jeremy Tankard. (Deal with it)

Includes bibliographical references.
ISBN-13: 978-1-55028-947-3
ISBN-10: 1-55028-947-0

1. Procrastination—Juvenile literature. I. Tankard, Jeremy II. Title. III. Series: Deal with it (Toronto, Ont.)

BF637.P76P47 2006 j155.2'32 C2006-903648-9

James Lorimer & Company Ltd., Publishers
317 Adelaide Street West, Suite #1002
Toronto, Ontario
M5V 1P9
www.lorimer.ca

Distributed in the United States by:
Orca Book Publishers
P.O. Box 468, Custer, WA
USA 98240-0468

Printed and bound in China